THE MOVIE NOVEL

METRO-GOLDWYN-MAYER PICTURES PRESENTS A JIM HENSON PICTURES PRODUCTION "GOOD BOY!" MOLLY SHANNON LIAM AIKEN KEVIN NEALON PRODUCER BILL BANNERMAN MUSIC BY MARK MOTHERSBAUGH EDITED BY CRAIG P. HERRING PRODUCTION DESIGNER JERRY WANEK DIRECTOR OF PHOTOGRAPHY JAMES GLENNON, ASC EXECUTIVE PRODUCER STEPHANIE ALLAIN PRODUCED BY LISA HENSON KRISTINE BELSON SCREEN STORY BY ZEKE RICHARDSON AND JOHN HOFFMAN SCREENPLAY BY JOHN HOFFMAN DIRECTED BY JOHN HOFFMAN DISTRIBUTED BY MGM DISTRIBUTION CO.

www.mgm.com

Good Boy!: The Movie Novel

Screen story by Zeke Richardson and John Hoffman
Based on the screenplay by John Hoffman

For information address HarperCollins Children's Books, a division of
HarperCollins Publishers, 1350 Avenue of the Americas, New York, NY 10019.
www.harperchildrens.com

Library of Congress catalog card number: 2003100109

Book design by Joe Merkel

1 2 3 4 5 6 7 8 9 10
❖
First Edition

THE MOVIE NOVEL

Written by Kathleen Weidner Zoehfeld
Based on the screenplay by John Hoffman
Screen story by Zeke Richardson
and John Hoffman

HarperFestival®
A Division of HarperCollins Publishers

CHAPTER 1

WHOOSH! A strange, small spacecraft glided across the starry sky. Owen Baker's telescope stood by his open window. His desk was piled high with books on astronomy and dogs. A few broken transistor radios sat awaiting repairs. But Owen was fast asleep. He snuggled under his covers and dreamed.

Whoosh, whoosh, whoosh—outside his window, the spacecraft zigzagged wildly. Whoever was piloting the craft was in serious trouble! *Whoosh, whoosh, whoooooooosssssssssssshhhhh* . . .

1

BOOM! A deep resounding vibration shook Owen from his dreams. His eyes snapped open. "What. . . ?"

Bzzzzzzzzzzzzzz. The Snoopy alarm clock on his night table announced it was time to get up for work. Owen slapped Snoopy's off-button nose and glanced around his room, confused. He spied the pile of new dog toys in the corner and smiled, forgetting all about the weird boom. Bounding out of bed, he tore the plastic wrapper off the new doggie bed and set it on the floor near the toys.

This was going to be a special day! He started his morning routine with an extra burst of energy. He put on his work clothes—maroon uniform, black shoes, dog-bone name tag—and his utility belt, equipped with doggie treats, brush, water bottle, and poop bags. One last check in the mirror to make sure his official orange cap was straight, and Owen was ready. *A little geeky, maybe*, he thought. *But sort of cool.*

On his dog calendar, big X's covered every day for the last three months. He pulled out his marker, popped off the cap, and X'ed one more, letting out a quick whoop of joy.

His parents were already up and at work painting and remodeling the den when he ran in to tell them the news.

"It's adoption day!" he cried.

"What?" gasped his mom, dropping her stenciling sponge.

"Hey, Owen," his dad greeted him calmly.

"It's 'stenciling day,' honey," corrected Mrs. Baker.

"Let me see that calendar," said Mr. Baker proudly.

"Didn't you just start that job?" queried Mrs. Baker.

"Ha, ha," said Owen, rolling his eyes.

"He's right," declared Mr. Baker. "It's exactly three months today he's been walking those dogs."

"And not one problem," said Owen. "I've got my dog already picked out at the shelter."

"Good for you, O," cheered Mr. Baker. "Great job!"

"Yes, absolutely. Terrific," said Mrs. Baker. "But, honey, let's chat for a second. Doesn't it make more sense to wait until we move to the new place before we get a dog?"

Owen scowled at her in silence.

Mrs. Baker squirmed. "I'm just thinking of the dog. That way, he won't have to relearn a new house and a new neighborhood and all of that other . . . newness."

"We had a deal, Mom."

"We did. We sure did," said Mrs. Baker, still uncertain.

Owen drew himself up in a parental posture. " 'The best way to achieve your dreams, Owen, is to make a plan, work hard, and always keep your eyes on the prize.' "

"That's an exact quote, isn't it?" asked Mrs. Baker.

"I want my prize," said Owen.

Mrs. Baker smiled. She had to admit it—she admired his determination. "Should we head over to the shelter at noon?"

Owen cheered, "Yes!"

They threw their arms around one another and hugged.

Owen's mom and dad watched from the den window as their only son trooped cheerfully off to work.

"A dog'll be good for him, right?" asked Mrs. Baker.

"A little buddy is just what he needs," declared Mr. Baker.

Mrs. Baker sighed. "I'd better put down some newspaper."

Owen walked up the path to his first house and rang the doorbell. "Morning, Ms. Ryan," he said.

"Mr. Baker," Ms. Ryan said elegantly. She smoothed back her well-coiffed hair with one hand. With the other she presented Owen the leash of her equally well-groomed white poodle. "Barbara Ann had a restless night, the poor dear," she gushed. "I don't want her overexerting herself today."

"I'll make sure she takes it easy," replied Owen.

"Keep her on the grass. The hot pavement is far too harsh on her delicate paws." Ms. Ryan watched like an anxious mother as Owen walked Barbara Ann down the street to the Healy residence.

Wilson, a bouncy, brown-and-white boxer, barked excitedly from behind the fence in his backyard. "Calm down, Wilson, it's only me," called Owen.

Wilson's "dad" was hurrying into his car to go to work. "He had the runs last night, Owen," he called. "Can you keep an eye on that for me? Let me know if things turn solid."

Owen grimaced as he clipped Wilson's leash on. "No problem."

Mr. Leone was already waiting at his door when Owen came trotting down the road with Wilson and Barbara Ann. The gray-haired gentleman cradled his skinny little Italian greyhound in his arms. "Be good, Nelly. Don't let the big dogs step on you."

"I'll watch out for her, Mr. Leone," said Owen sympathetically.

"I know you will," said Mr. Leone.

Connie Fleming's dog, Shep, started wagging his tail frantically as soon as he spotted Owen and his crew of three coming around the bend. Connie, one of Owen's schoolmates, was hanging on her front porch with two friends.

"Connie, here comes your boyfriend," teased Franky.

"Direct from Weirdoville," echoed the dim-witted Fred.

"Cut it out," said Connie.

"Good morning, Franky, Fred," said Owen.

"Good morning, loser," sneered Franky.

Connie bent down to hug her big Bernese mountain dog. "Gimme a kiss good-bye, Shep. Gimme a kiss!"

Shep covered Connie's face in sloppy dog kisses.

Owen asked Connie if she wanted to come along.

"Why do you wear those stupid clothes?" demanded Franky.

"Because all my smart clothes are in the laundry," quipped Owen. "You coming, Connie?"

"We're going to the pool," she said.

Franky waved his towel in front of Owen's eyes by way of demonstration. "Duh, dog-boy."

Fred sniffed. "I smell poop."

Wilson looked up at Owen sheepishly. "Aw, Wilson," Owen sighed. "Well, at least it's solid. . . ." He pulled out a poop bag and scooped up Wilson's mess, while the boys made a wide circle around him and climbed onto their bikes.

"Gross," said Fred.

"You coming, Connie?" called Franky.

But Connie held back. "Aren't you getting your dog today?" she asked Owen.

Owen pretended not to care that she'd

decided to go to the pool with those lamebrains instead of walking the dogs with him. "Yep. So . . . I probably won't be seeing you around much anymore."

"You'll still walk Shep, though. Right?"

"Yeah, well, I'll see you *then*," Owen corrected himself. "But otherwise I'll be really busy with training and getting my dog used to his new home. Bonding with him and all that."

Connie watched as Owen started off with the dogs.

"Connie, move your butt!" yelled Franky.

"Have fun at the pool," said Owen over his shoulder as he let the exuberant dogs lead him away.

CHAPTER

2

Owen and his crew—Barbara Ann, Wilson, Nelly, and Shep—were headed onto a quiet woodsy road for a nice long stroll when Owen spotted something up ahead. He stopped immediately. Just up the road on the other side, a brown-haired mutt sat staring at them.

"Where'd you come from?" asked Owen.

The strange dog lifted one paw and studied them. Then he let out a weird, unearthly howl. The dogs bolted in terror. Owen, holding a firm grip on their leashes, nearly toppled over.

As Owen regained his composure, the strange mutt moved slowly toward him. "Hey, boy. You lost?" Owen asked. He reached down to pat the dog's head. Suddenly, the dog reared up on his hind legs and let out a loud bark that sounded like a drill sergeant's command to his troops.

"Jeez!" cried Owen. His dogs began to run frantically, trying to get away from the stranger, tangling and winding their leashes around Owen in the process.

"Wait! Stop!" cried Owen. Round and round the dogs ran, wrapping him tighter and tighter until—*Wham!*—he fell over and hit the ground, with the dogs all in a heap on top of him.

Owen saw a proud, triumphant look in the mutt's dark eyes. He was going to pounce! Owen cringed, ready for the attack. . . .

Bob, the dogcatcher from the animal shelter, had been cruising the area in his van, looking for strays, when he spotted Owen in trouble. Just in the nick of time, he lassoed the loop of a brace stick around the strange dog's neck and stopped him in his tracks. "Gotcha!" cried Bob.

"Thanks," said Owen, freeing himself from the tangle of leashes.

"See you at the shelter this afternoon?" Bob asked as he locked the growling mutt in his van.

"Yep," said Owen. "Today's the day!"

As soon as he'd returned his charges to their owners, Owen hurried home. The Baker family piled into their car, and Owen's mom held up her camera to document the big occasion. "Somebody's about to meet his new best friend," she sang.

Owen blushed as his mother snapped his picture.

At the animal shelter, a couple of women were already checking out the dogs. "Look at this one! Who's the pretty boy?" crooned one of the women, spotting the brown-haired mutt Bob had just brought in.

The mutt let out a deep rumbling growl and bared his sharp white teeth.

"Dang!" cried the other woman. "Pretty nasty!"

In the opposite cage a cute little Westie whimpered.

"Adorable!" said the first woman.

"Gimme kisses, gimme some kisses," cried the other.

Bob opened the Westie's cage and let them play. The Westie covered them in kisses and wiggled and wagged his tail happily. Meanwhile, the strange mutt eyed them from his cage. He saw the Westie being carried off by his new owners. *Hmmm . . . cute and cuddly equals freedom,* the mutt thought. He was a quick learner.

Owen and his parents were standing before a cage with a sign that said:

ON HOLD FOR BAKER.

Inside sat a quiet, mild-mannered basset hound. "You're sure *this* is the one?" asked his mom.

"My book said basset hounds are obedient, loyal, and make wonderful companions," said Owen.

"Did your book say anything about fun?" his mother asked.

From a few kennels down, Owen heard a familiar howl. He turned and saw the strange mutt from the woods.

The mutt put on the sweetest look he could muster. He cocked his head longingly and gave Owen a little woof.

"Wow," said Mr. Baker. "Now, *he's* interesting."

"Poor little prisoner," said Mrs. Baker.

"Hey," called Bob as he spotted Owen, "there's the man! Did you tell your folks about your scuffle this morning?"

"What?" exclaimed Mr. and Mrs. Baker.

"Owen helped me nab this tough mutt off the streets," Bob explained.

"Tough?" asked Mr. Baker. "Is he a stray?"

"There are no tags on him," said Bob, "just that funny rock hanging from a string around his neck. He checked out all right healthwise, though."

"He seems worried about something," said

Owen, moving closer to the cage.

"I'd be worried too," said Bob. "His days are numbered, I think. That attitude of his isn't making him too popular around here."

"You won't put him to sleep, will you?" asked Owen.

"We've only got so much room, and if nobody wants him . . ." Bob shrugged helplessly.

Realizing his desperate situation, the mutt played cutesy with the Bakers. He rolled on his back and snuzzled his furry snout in his paws. He covered his eyes and started playing peekaboo.

"Aw . . . peekaboo! Peekaboo, puppy!" crooned Mr. and Mrs. Baker, getting into the game themselves.

The mutt gave them a fetching wink. Mrs. Baker took a photgraph.

Over by the basset hound's cage a little boy fought back tears. "But I like this one best, Daddy," Owen heard the little boy whine.

"Son, I told you, he's already on hold for someone else," said the boy's father.

Owen looked at the troublemaking brown-haired mutt and made the decision of his life. "We'll take him," he told Bob.

Later, at home with his new "pal," Owen tried to remove the strange rock hanging around the dog's neck. The mutt growled at him.

"It's all right," said Owen, getting the point. "You can keep it. Just let me put it on your nice new collar. There . . . "

The mutt calmed down a little and started exploring Owen's room.

"Here's your bed, boy. Right here. Nice, huh?" said Owen. He patted the dog's head.

"*Grrrrrrrrrr*," the dog growled menacingly.

"Whoa," cried Owen, pulling his hand away.

In a huff, the mutt trotted to the window and checked out the view.

"Okay . . . " said Owen, gathering his courage. He could see this dog was going to take some getting used to. "I've got to give you a name."

He grabbed one of the new squeaky toys. "You tell me which name you like. Here, Armstrong! Wanna squeaky, Armstrong?"

The dog shook his head in annoyance, making his ears flap like flags in a rough wind.

"Okay, Armstrong's lame, I know. How about Apollo? C'mon, Apollo!"

This time the mutt just ignored him. He was more interested in Owen's telescope. He hopped up on Owen's desk, leaned toward the eyepiece, and put one of his eyes up to it.

Owen stared in amazement. "What the . . ."

Adjusting the telescope's angle to the right a little, the mutt seemed satisfied. He let out one of his out-of-this-world howls, while one of his ears unfolded and stood straight up.

On Owen's desk, next to his totally bizarre new dog, lay one of his favorite books: *The Wonders of the Hubble Telescope.*

Hubble, thought Owen. *His name'll be Hubble.*

CHAPTER 3

"Hubble! Slow down. Heel, Hubble. Heel!" cried Owen as they rushed to the dog park the next day, with Hubble in the lead.

Hubble tugged Owen through the gate and trotted toward Mr. Leone, who was sitting on a park bench reading his newspaper.

"Hey, Mr. Leone," said Owen.

"Hello there. And who is this?" asked Mr. Leone kindly.

"His name's Hubble. I just got him."

"Well, hello, Hubble. Welcome . . ."

Hubble growled and sneered, baring his sharp teeth.

"Oops!" cried Mr. Leone.

"No, Hubble! No!" commanded Owen.

"It's all right. I'm a stranger to him."

"Where's Nelly?" asked Owen. He unclipped Hubble's leash to let him run in the fenced-in grassy area. Little Nelly peeked out cautiously from around Mr. Leone's newspaper.

"She likes to check the headlines," said Mr. Leone. He patted her fondly.

Suddenly Hubble charged up to Nelly and barked in her face. Nelly jumped and took off like a rocket, with Hubble chasing after her.

"Hubble, no!" cried Owen desperately. "Sorry. I've got to train him."

"Well, good luck with that!" cried Mr. Leone, rushing to rescue his Nelly from Hubble's charge.

After Mr. Leone brought Nelly back to safety they huddled together on the park bench again, while Owen tried out some new commands with his unpredictable dog.

"Sit," said Owen.

With his eyes still glued menacingly on Nelly, Hubble sat.

"Good boy!" cried Owen in complete surprise.

Mr. Leone nodded and smiled.

"Stay. Hubble, stay!" commanded Owen.

Practically yawning with boredom, Hubble stayed put.

"He is a bright one!" cried Mr. Leone.

Owen was confused. How could this crazy stray know these commands? He tried something even harder. "Okay, Mr. Genius. How about . . . roll over?"

Slowly, Hubble crouched to the ground, pushed with his paws, and rolled over on his back.

Now Owen was truly freaked. "Play dead?" he tried.

Hubble trotted a short distance away, slowed down, stumbled, rose up on his hind legs, wove around in a few dizzy circles, and plopped dramatically to the ground, falling on his back, his legs sticking straight up in the air.

Nelly buried her nose in Mr. Leone's armpit. Mr. Leone sat in silent astonishment.

Owen rushed home with Hubble to tell his dad about their weird afternoon in the dog park. His father had just finished installing the doggie door-flap on their back door.

"He's *really* smart, Dad!" cried Owen.

"That's terrific, O," said Mr. Baker.

"No," said Owen, "I mean . . . he's *too* smart."

"Son, I hate to break it to you, but everyone thinks they've got the smartest dog in the universe."

Well, maybe, thought Owen. But when he went to his bedroom, one look told him otherwise. Hubble was already sitting at his desk— studying an encyclopedia!

Maybe there was something about dogs he didn't know. He pulled out a book about pets and started reading. "There are few things more powerful than the bond of love and loyalty between a dog and his master," the book began. Owen wondered about Hubble. Would this dog ever feel love and loyalty toward him?

He watched Hubble move to the corner near his doggie bed. He sat facing the wall. Owen went up to him and gently tried to pat his head, but Hubble backed away and growled.

"All right," said Owen. "We'll take our time."

Owen went back to his bed, trying to act unconcerned. Once Owen was out of the way, Hubble inched closer to his own bed and sniffed it. He circled it twice then seemed to settle down for the night. Owen sighed and snapped off the light.

A few hours went by as Hubble pretended to sleep. Then, slowly, he crept out of his doggie bed.

Owen heard the creak of his door swinging open. He sat up and, peering in the dim light, saw that Hubble's bed was empty.

He ran out to the hallway whispering, "Hubble?"

He rushed downstairs to the kitchen just in time to see the doggie flap swinging on the back door. Through the window he spotted Hubble walking off down the block.

Owen jumped into his sneakers, put his jacket on over his pajamas, and grabbed a flashlight. In seconds he was following close behind.

Hubble headed for the woods. He knew exactly where he was going. Once through a dense, brushy area, he could see the familiar hill where his spacecraft had crashed to earth. He made a beeline for the old oak tree on the hilltop.

Spotting the mound of dirt where he'd buried his damaged equipment, he began to dig frantically. There it was! He pulled a broken radio out of the ground. Desperately, he fiddled with the controls, hoping to re-establish the communications link with his home world.

Meanwhile, Owen hurried through the woods after him. He pushed through the thicket of branches, pulling leaves from his hair and spitting sticky cobwebs from his mouth. When he reached the clearing, he spotted Hubble on the hilltop. He started climbing.

"*Pssssssssssshhhhhhhhhhhhhhhhhhh weeeeeeeeeewwoooooooooooo . . .*"

Owen stopped short. He heard snippets of radio messages: ". . . on sale this week at Anderson's, fresh ripe peaches . . . *weeeeeeeeeeeeeeeeeeeeeeee ooooooooooo* . . . We're your power station, KRZY. Crazy for classic rock . . . *pssssssssshhhhhhhhhh* . . . *weeeeeeeeooooo* . . . I tell you miracles are happening every day in our world. You just need to look . . . *ppsssssssssssssssssh* . . ."

Suddenly a beam of bright light shot from Hubble's radio to the sky. Owen heard Hubble let out one of his strange howls. Then the clouds began to roll away. Hubble's antenna ear unfolded.

Grrrrrrrrrrrrrrrrrrrrrmmmmmmmmmmmmm . . . .

The radio announcements were replaced by a deep rumbling tone. A tapping like Morse code and the sounds of barking dogs began to fill the air.

Owen struggled against the whipping wind to climb closer to Hubble. "Here, boy . . ." he called weakly through the uproar.

Hubble turned and spotted him. Too late! *ZZZZZZZaaaaappp! Crrrrrrrrraaaaaaaaaaaaaakkk!* Hubble's radio short-circuited, sending a huge, blinding flash of light around the entire hilltop.

Owen sat up in his bed, bewildered. "That was a weird dream," he mumbled. He shook his head and looked over at Hubble, who was awake and staring at him from his bed.

"What did I get myself into with you?" asked Owen. He settled back down to sleep, turning away from Hubble.

"How do you think I feel?" came a voice from the corner.

Owen's eyes popped open. What was he hearing?

"Roll over?" said the voice.

Owen rolled over and faced Hubble.

"Sit?"

This time Owen distinctly saw his dog say the word! Owen sat up.

"You hear me?" asked Hubble.

"I . . . I . . ." stammered Owen.

"You're sure?"

"Uh-huh."

"Doggone it!" cried Hubble. "How could I let this happen? Don't be afraid . . . I am Canid Three-Nine-Four-Two."

"Honey!" Owen heard Mrs. Baker calling him from downstairs. He fell off his bed.

"Time to be up and at 'em!" she called.

Owen sprang to his feet and ran to the opposite side of the room—his eyes fixed on Hubble.

Mrs. Baker popped her head in the door. "You can't forget about the other dogs just because you've got Hubble now," she said.

Hubble sneezed a perfectly normal doggie sneeze.

"Aw . . . gesundheit." She patted Hubble.

"Hop to it, O!" she called as she headed back downstairs.

Owen stared at his talking dog.

"What?" asked Hubble, annoyed. "I have allergies."

Without once taking his eyes off the dog, Owen pulled on his work clothes and clipped on Hubble's leash. Hubble practically dragged Owen out of the house.

"Did you just learn how to talk?" whispered Owen urgently.

"Here come the questions," sighed Hubble. "Let's just say your hearing suddenly got a lot better."

"Oh, man!" cried Owen. "How is this even possible?"

"Look, you run a fine hotel, but I don't have time to train you right now. Just take me to your leaders," demanded Hubble.

"Leaders?" asked Owen.

"The dogs who walk you," explained Hubble.

"The dogs who walk *me*? I walk *them*."

"Sure you do," said Hubble, like a detective sweet-talking an uncooperative witness. "I'll get to the bottom of this."

"Wait, am I the only one who can understand you?"

Hubble stopped and faced him. "Yes," he said. "And I know the communication barrier must never be broken. You can't tell anyone about this—ever! Got it? I could be in deep doo-doo."

Owen scoffed at Hubble's concern. "Nobody would believe me anyway. Dogs don't just start *talking* all of a sudden."

CHAPTER 5

"Who is this new guy, anyway? I don't like this!
I feel violated. My whole sense of privacy,
completely violated . . ." Yap, yap, yap, yap, yap.
Owen's muttly crew had been chattering and
complaining among themselves all morning. And
they were driving him crazy!

"*Aaaaaaaaaaaaaahhhhhhhhh!*" he cried as
they dragged him down the road. He had to get
the dogs off the street and figure out what was
going on.

"C'mon, guys." Owen coaxed the grumpy

crew into his garage for a private meeting. Checking the window to make sure they weren't being watched, he pulled down the shade and switched on the overhead light. The dogs milled around nervously, sniffing at the birdhouses and other crafts that Mr. Baker made in his wood-working shop.

Wilson hopped up on one of Mr. Baker's worktables and looked Owen in the eye. "You can really understand me? Right now, you understand what I'm saying to you?"

"Yep," replied Owen.

Wilson got right in Owen's face. "Can I have a cookie? No wait, ten cookies. Can I have twenty cookies?"

"Oh, I have dreamed of talking to people since I was paper trained," tittered Nelly. "Where do I start?"

"Be a pal, kid," said Shep. "Loosen my collar a notch. I've got a *foof* in my *chach*!"

"Owen, honey, be honest," gushed Barbara Ann. "Does this pink bow make me look fat?"

"Oh—oh—oh," stammered Nelly, "I'm so nervous I can't think of a thing to say."

"I know," quipped Wilson. "Can you teach us how to use a can opener?"

"That's a good one," said Shep. "Hey, I got another one for you—two pit bulls and a wiener dog walk into a kennel—"

Before Shep could finish his joke, Hubble climbed up on a box and shouted, "Enough! Collect yourselves."

"I guess he heard that one already," said Shep.

The dogs gathered and looked up at Hubble uneasily.

"Which one of you is the alpha dog?" he asked.

From their blank looks, Hubble could see none of them had a clue what he was talking about.

"Fine," huffed Hubble. "Who is responsible for the alpha-dog duties?"

"I make nice doodies," offered Nelly.

Hubble harrumphed in annoyance. "I have

come here on an important mission from the home star, and I expect full cooperation."

"Hold it," cried Owen. "Where are you from?"

"Where we *all* came from," sighed Hubble impatiently. He pulled at the window shade with his teeth and let it snap up. "The home star!" he declared, pointing his muzzle to the sky.

"Oh my gosh. It's true! I knew it! Unbelievable!" the dogs all gasped and started chattering at once.

"What are you talking about?" demanded Owen.

"Thousands of years ago dogs arrived here from the home star to colonize and dominate the planet. All Earth dogs are descended from those dogs," recited Hubble in a bored tone. "Everyone knows this."

"What home star?" asked Owen.

"It's Sirius," said Hubble.

"So, you can't tell me?"

"I just did," said Hubble.

"Did what?"

"Told you."

"You said it was serious."

"That's right," said Hubble.

"And that's why you can't tell me?"

"Sweet biscuits," cried Barbara Ann, "we'll be here all night!"

"This reminds me of a funny bit I once did with a Chihuahua named Mitzi," the comedian, Shep, chimed in.

"I'm just asking a simple question," whined Owen.

"This is why dogs and people shouldn't talk," sighed Hubble.

Wilson leaned over and whispered in Owen's ear, "Dude, the name of the star is Sirius."

"Oh, *that* Sirius—the Dog Star!" Owen did a double take. "Wait, Wilson, you *know* about this?"

"I heard about it," said Wilson. "I didn't know it was real."

"My grandma used to tell me stories," said Nelly.

"Sure, we've all heard them," agreed Shep.

"Sirius puppy tales."

"Hubble, you expect me to believe there's a planet out there ruled by dogs?" demanded Owen.

"We don't expect much from your species. Now go outside and play so we can do our business. Go on—go play!" shouted Hubble.

"I don't have to go outside!" Owen shouted back.

Seeing a bad situation brewing, Shep interrupted. "Pardon me, but you were saying something about a mission?"

"Right. Thank you," harrumphed Hubble, getting back to business. "I have been sent here to file a report on Earth dogs."

"A report?" asked Owen. "What, like a report card?"

"Yes," barked Hubble. "Now *sit*!"

Owen sat obediently as Hubble turned back to the crew.

"I'm not sure what's happening on this planet, but I intend to find out," said Hubble. "You will be my official test group."

"We're going to represent all Earth dogs?" asked Wilson.

"That's right," said Hubble. "I will observe your lives and then grade you on how you've upheld the Sirius code of dignity and dominance."

"We're going to get graded?" fretted Nelly.

"Yes!" exclaimed Hubble.

"I got all A's at Miss Bonnie's Canine Academy," boasted Barbara Ann.

"Then you'll be happy to hear I'll be submitting my report directly to Our Most Noble Pack Leader—the Greater Dane!" declared Hubble.

The dogs gasped.

"The top dog?" asked Wilson.

"Canine-in-Chief," said Hubble.

"I need to pee-pee," whined Nelly.

"The Greater Dane is troubled by rumors floating around the galaxy that Earth dogs have lost control of this planet," said Hubble.

The dogs looked at each other sheepishly. Shep gulped.

"How . . . bizarre?" burbled Barbara Ann, trying to cover for them.

"Yeah," agreed Wilson. "Who would say a thing like that?"

"Hold on," said Owen. "You don't seriously think dogs are in charge of—"

"Can we get some air?" interrupted Nelly. "I feel woozy."

By the time they reached the dog park, Owen was steaming. He and Hubble stood face-to-face near the old fountain. The crew leaned in close to hear what they were saying.

"See this?" said Owen, holding out Hubble's leash. "I bought it. I clip it on you because you are *my* dog. I *own* you."

Wilson whispered in Hubble's ear nervously, "He's a funny guy, isn't he?"

"People own dogs—not the other way around!" shouted Owen.

"We like to make them feel that way," said Barbara Ann sweetly.

"Yeah, it pumps them up," said Wilson.

"Makes them easier to tame," said Shep.

Hubble considered what the dogs were saying.

But Owen was not about to give in to their nonsense. "The idea of dogs being in charge is so far-fetched—"

"Fetch?" Wilson's ears perked up and a joyful gleam came into his eyes. He bounced off into the grassy area and shouted to Owen, "Dude! I'm open! Toss me the ball! I'm totally open here!"

Owen ignored Wilson and gestured wildly at Hubble. "Dogs obey people because people are a lot smarter. Get it?"

Owen was so involved in his argument, he didn't notice that an audience had gathered. Connie and her two pals, Franky and Fred, were biking past when they caught sight of Owen. And he was acting stranger than ever. The dogs were barking, and he was talking back to them as though they were having a conversation!

"Baker! Who are you talking to?" cried Franky.

"Yeah, who?" echoed Fred.

Owen wheeled around, startled. "Huh? Oh . . . just the dogs."

"You're talking to them like they're people," sneered Franky.

"You've got to—to train them," said Owen lamely.

"Let's just go, you guys," said Connie, embarrassed.

"Connie, I wouldn't let *my* dog hang out with that mental case," advised Franky.

"What a mental," echoed Fred.

Connie looked back at Owen as they rode away. *What was with him lately, anyway?* she wondered. *Why was he acting so weird?*

CHAPTER 6

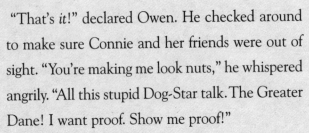

"That's *it*!" declared Owen. He checked around to make sure Connie and her friends were out of sight. "You're making me look nuts," he whispered angrily. "All this stupid Dog-Star talk. The Greater Dane! I want proof. Show me proof!"

Hubble raised his eyebrows disdainfully. "Heel!" he cried.

As they scrambled through the brushy woods, Owen realized Hubble was leading them to the hilltop in last night's dream. Under the familiar oak tree they found a deep hole in the earth.

Owen peered in and saw a small, disk-shaped spacecraft.

"Works for me," he said. Now he had to believe Hubble's story.

Hubble hopped into the hole and tried to open the cockpit.

"You know how to drive?" asked Nelly, full of admiration.

"He knows how to crash," quipped Wilson.

Hubble scowled. "I'm an excellent pilot. There just happened to be some radical wind currents the other night, and . . ."

Suddenly Owen spotted the radio he'd seen in his dream. "What's this?" he interrupted.

"Be careful," cried Hubble. "That's my woofer."

"Huh?"

"A communicator," explained Hubble.

"Ah . . ."

"It got slightly damaged in the landing," said Hubble.

"Slightly?" cried Wilson. The thing was a mess.

Hubble gave him a look.

Owen examined the radio. "This is what you were using last night when—"

"Yes, when it short-circuited and you were caught in the current, don't remind me. Now I'm talking to *you*, but I can't contact Sirius."

"I bet I can fix this," said Owen.

"Keep your paws off my woofer," growled Hubble.

"No, I'm good with this stuff," said Owen. "Really. I couldn't make it any worse."

"Fine, that'll be your job," ordered Hubble. "As for the rest of you, tomorrow I start grading. I'll want to see all the ways you've taken control of people and the planet."

"Yeah." Owen laughed. "I want to see that too."

Far from having taken control, the dogs seemed to have a lot of complaints. Owen figured the least he could do—as the top life-form on the planet (so far)—was to let their owners know some of the stuff they'd said today. When he returned them late that morning, he told Ms. Ryan that Barbara Ann preferred the pavement to the grass because she was afraid of bugs. Shep, he said, wanted Connie to know that he liked his collar a notch looser. Nelly wanted to tell Mr. Leone that she would rather start her daily reading with the comics, because the headlines made her nervous. And Wilson's upset stomach—well, that was caused by the new vitamins his "dad" was putting in his food.

The dog's owners were taken aback. What was happening with Owen? Was he becoming clairvoyant, or was he making all this stuff up? How did he know so much about their precious pets?

That evening, Owen set himself up at his father's carpentry table and got to work on the broken woofer. He poked at it with a screwdriver and it broke in two.

"Whoops," he said.

"If you don't know what you're doing—" snapped Hubble.

"Gimme a chance!" cried Owen.

"You've *got* to fix that. I'll be the laughing-stock of Sirius," groaned Hubble.

"Ha, ha," said Owen dryly.

"What?"

"You made a joke. The *laughingstock* of *Sirius?*"

"Just fix my woofer," scowled Hubble.

"Chill out, Hubble."

"My *name* is Canid Three-Nine-Four-Two."

"I'm not calling you by some number," said Owen. "I named you Hubble."

Hubble flopped on the floor and sprawled all four legs out sideways. He figured this conversation was going to take a while. "When did these human-dog relationships start, anyway?" he asked.

"Thousands of years ago," said Owen.

"But why? Why on earth would we do that?"

"Hubble, believe it or not, dogs here are called

'Man's best friend.'"

"Friend?" cried Hubble. "Dogs don't need friends!"

"Everybody needs friends."

"Why?"

"Well, I'm probably not the best person to ask," said Owen. "I don't really have any."

Owen's dad tapped lightly at the door and peeked in. "Hey, you two having a chat in here?" He chuckled.

"Yeah. Ha, ha . . ." Owen laughed self-consciously. He put the woofer aside so his father wouldn't notice it.

"Hey there, little guy," said Mr. Baker, stroking Hubble's head.

Hubble backed away, nearly upsetting a canister of toxic paint sealant in the process.

"Whoa! Careful!" cried Mr. Baker, catching the canister before it hit the ground. "Knock that over and the fumes will knock us out."

Owen could see that his dad had something to say. They looked at one another for a moment.

"So . . ." Mr. Baker started, "Mom and I are finishing up in the den tomorrow."

"Hmm," grunted Owen.

"Yep, then it's moving time again. I think this has been my favorite house so far."

"Mine too," said Owen quietly.

"You okay?" asked Mr. Baker.

"I'm okay."

"Okeydoke, then. Sleep tight, kiddo. And you too, stubborn Hubble." Mr. Baker petted him.

Hubble growled.

"Hey, I think he understood me!" Mr. Baker laughed.

"Heh, heh." Owen pretended to laugh along.

"*Rrrrrrrr,*" grumbled Hubble when Mr. Baker had gone. "If one more person wipes his hands on me—"

"Come on," said Owen. "We'd better get some rest." He wrapped the woofer in an old cloth, and they shuffled up the stairs.

From his bed, Owen watched as Hubble circled his doggie bed twice and then settled in.

"Why do you do that?" he asked.

"Because I need sleep," said Hubble.

"No, why do you turn around like that?"

"Enough with the questions!" cried Hubble. "We've got a busy day tomorrow. Lights out."

Owen hit the switch and lay back in bed. His eyes stayed wide-open, though. And his mind was racing. "Hubble?" he asked.

"*Rrrrrrrr.*"

"Just one more," said Owen. "How could dogs run a whole planet all on their own? I mean, no offense, but you guys don't have that much intelligence."

Hubble raised his head from his paws. "Oh, really? Haven't I spent all day teaching *you* things you didn't know anything about?"

"You may know about where *you* live," said Owen, annoyed, "but I know a lot about where I live. And one thing I know is—dogs don't run things!"

CHAPTER 7

"Wait till you see the way we got things running down here!" bragged Shep the next morning.

The dogs milled around the fountain in the dog park. They were too excited to sit still—this was their chance to convince Hubble that they had not completely failed in their mission to take over the Earth.

"It's really quite fabulous," gushed Barbara Ann.

"Yeah, right," said Owen sarcastically.

"I'm not shaking because I'm nervous," said

Nelly. "I'm shaking because I'm excited."

"Earth dogs rule, dude!" cried Wilson.

"On Tuesdays, I like to visit Lady Evelyn for my bubble bath, massage, manicure, and trim," explained Barbara Ann. "She costs a bit more, but I'm worth it." Barbara Ann showed off her big pink bow and perfectly brushed white curls. "Such a pretty bow. Such a pretty me! Good grooming is essential to good ruling."

"Poor people," agreed Wilson. "They work like dogs—so we don't have to. My humans keep my yard and garden just right for running and digging and rolling. I taught them everything they know."

"Sometimes you just need to get away—let your ears down and catch a breeze," said Shep, daydreaming of long car rides with the windows down. "I don't know where I'd be without my chauffeur."

"And they *have* to scratch us," said Nelly. "That's the deal."

"Everything at my house is mine," added

Wilson. "I have a stoop. That's mine. Some bushes. Those are mine. I have a little fence. That's definitely mine. Oh, yeah, and a nifty mailbox . . ." Wilson's list went on and on. He lifted his hind leg at the mention of every item, demonstrating for Hubble how he put his "signature" on each one.

"We do what we want," declared Wilson.

"We get what we want," added Nelly.

"We *go* where we want," said Barbara Ann.

"And let's face it," concluded Shep, "you don't see us picking up *their* poop."

"Okay, that last one got me," conceded Owen.

"Pretty cool, huh?" asked Wilson. He turned to Hubble. "So, what do *you* think, Mr. Spacedog?"

Hubble stood on the fountain wall and faced the expectant crew. "You've gone native!" he declared.

"Is that good?" asked Nelly.

"You are all in so much trouble!" cried Hubble.

"Nope. It's bad," said Wilson.

Owen saw the worried looks on their faces. "Come on," he pleaded, "how much trouble can they really be in?"

"Trust me," snapped Hubble. *"You don't want to know."* He glowered at the dogs. "Lazy, greedy, spoiled-rottens! You've lost all dignity!"

"Will this affect our report cards?" asked Nelly.

"What do you think!?" growled Hubble.

Out of the blue, a high-pitched whistle blared.

"There's that noise again," said Nelly, scratching an ear with her hind paw.

Wilson and Shep scratched their ears too. Owen had to cover his.

"That's just awful!" declared Barbara Ann, shaking her head.

"What are you doing?" demanded Hubble.

Wilson grimaced. "This happens a couple of times every day."

"We just try to ignore it," said Shep.

"*That* is Sirius calling!" cried Hubble as the

noise faded. "No wonder we haven't heard from Earth dogs in years. You've forgotten everything! I've got no choice—I have to flunk you."

The dogs drooped.

"Flunk them?" asked Owen.

"Pardon me," said Shep, "but we've been away from the home star so long. Maybe if you were to help refresh our memory a little . . ."

"Yes!" cried Nelly. "Be our teacher!"

"That's not my job," said Hubble. "I make my report, and I go."

"Go? What do you mean . . . go?" asked Owen.

"Mission Command will send a retriever for me . . . eventually," said Hubble.

Owen's heart sank. He sat quietly on the side of the fountain while the dogs chattered nervously.

"So we still have some time to improve," declared Shep.

"Please help us, Hubble," begged Nelly. "We don't want to flunk."

"I've been a blue-ribbon girl all my life," boasted Barbara Ann.

"Yeah! We want to be more like *you*," gushed Wilson.

"Absolutely!" agreed Barbara Ann. "Intelligent, dignified—"

"Who are we kidding?" sighed Nelly. "We could only *dream* of being as dignified as Hubble."

"Well, I don't know about that," he protested in a humble tone.

"I may be an old dog, but I like to learn new tricks," claimed Shep.

"Please? Oh, please, please, please?" Wilson put his head down between his front paws and groveled.

Hubble surveyed them from his perch on the fountain wall. "I usually don't approve of begging . . ." He looked over at Owen, "but I *could* teach them a thing or two."

The dogs bounced and wiggled and wagged their tails in celebration. "Yay! Hot diggity! You the dog! Hubble rocks! We're not going to flunk!

We're not going to flunk!" they all cheered.

"But no funny business, understand?" commanded Hubble. "Tomorrow, you start getting Sirius!"

After Owen and Hubble had escorted the dogs back to their houses for the day, they strolled quietly home together, each thinking their own thoughts about the morning's events.

"I didn't realize I'd made such an impression on them," mused Hubble. "They really seem to look up to me."

"That's the thing about Earth dogs, Hub—if they like you, they're not afraid to let you know."

Deep in conversation, Owen and Hubble didn't notice Franky and Fred making faces at them from the barbershop window. Just as Owen was about to look in, the barber, Franky's father, shouted for the boys to quit it and sit down for their haircuts.

"Hold on, what's this?" asked Hubble as they moved past the barbershop. He gestured to a mannequin in a nearby window.

"That's a store. Where you buy things," explained Owen.

"How much is that person in the window?" asked Hubble.

Owen shot him a look. Was he serious?

As soon as they reached their front door, Owen's mom motioned him excitedly into the den. She switched on the lights. "Ta-da!"

"Wow . . ." said Owen.

"I know, finally," sighed Mrs. Baker. "Now we can get started on the new place in Metro Village." She got her camera out and started taking pictures of the room.

"So soon?" asked Owen.

"It's our dream home, honey," said Mrs. Baker. "I can't wait to get in there and get to work."

"That's what you said about this house, Mom. And the house before that, and the one before that . . ."

"It's what we do, honey."

"I know, I just wish we could *stay* somewhere for good."

"It just makes more sense financially to live in the house we're renovating," Mrs. Baker tried to explain. "And every time we move, we get a nicer place, right?"

"This place seems nice enough to me," said Owen.

"Thank you, sweetie. That's a lovely compliment, but I bet you'll like the new house best of all." She stroked his chin lovingly. "And this time you won't be starting off all alone, right? You'll have Hubble!"

Owen nodded. *Sure,* he thought, *I get the dog who doesn't plan to stay.* He slumped out to the front porch to watch the stars come out.

Hubble was sitting patiently on the porch swing, waiting. He wagged his tail. "Where were you?" he asked.

"With my mom," said Owen. "Why do you care?"

"I don't know," said Hubble. "For some reason I was afraid that you were never coming back."

Owen plopped down on the swing and sighed. Hubble inched a teensy bit closer. They watched the full moon come up over the trees across the street.

"Why do dogs howl at the moon?" asked Owen.

"Only coyotes do that," explained Hubble. "But it's not the moon—they're howling to the home star."

"Sirius?"

"Just to the left. Two stars over. Coyotes are homesick crybabies."

Owen smiled a little. "So . . . when that retriever you talked about comes for you—you're planning on going back with him?"

"This is only a temporary mission," said Hubble.

"Right. I get it," said Owen, pretending not to care.

"I appreciate your hosting me for the time being, but—"

"It's okay," Owen stopped him. "I'm used to temporary missions."

CHAPTER 9

The next morning at the park, Hubble began the dogs' training. For their first lesson, he asked them to lie on their backs in a row, their eyes closed, legs sprawled out to their sides.

He paced among them, addressing them serenely: "Dignity comes from within. On Sirius, we begin every day with meditation. Breathe in, and out. Relax. Let it go. . . ."

Shep farted. "Pardon me," he muttered.

"Shep gets people food sometimes," tittered Nelly.

"How lucky for us," sighed Hubble.

Owen sat and watched, stifling a laugh. In the baseball field nearby, Franky was getting up to bat. Fred wound up to pitch. Connie crouched behind the plate and held her catcher's glove ready.

"This one's out of the park!" cried Franky, taking a practice swing.

Wilson's eyes popped open. Shep's ears twitched. Nelly and Barbara Ann quivered.

"Erase all distractions from your mind," said Hubble.

Thwop! Franky walloped the rubber ball. It flew out of the ballpark and bounced past Hubble's head.

"*Focus* is the key to canine composure," said Hubble evenly.

Before he knew it, four crazed canines had trampled him in their wild stampede for the ball. Knocked dizzy and spitting dirt, Hubble struggled to his feet, bewildered. "What's the matter with all of you?"

Owen couldn't help laughing. He pointed to

Wilson, who was trotting back proudly with the ball in his mouth.

"Baker! Give me back my ball," demanded Franky.

"Yeah, give it," echoed Fred.

Owen shrugged. "I don't have it."

"Why don't you *talk* to your dogs and tell them to give it back," sneered Franky.

"Yeah, *talk* to them, dog-boy," said Fred.

Owen looked at Connie, but she avoided his glance. How could she stand hanging with these deadbeats?

Hubble let out one of his weird, Dog-Star howls.

"What a freak!" cried Franky.

"Yeah, your dog's a freak like you," said Fred.

Franky started picking up pebbles and whipping them at Hubble.

"Don't!" cried Owen.

Soon, Fred was throwing pebbles too.

"You guys!" cried Connie in annoyance.

"Quit it!" yelled Owen.

"Who's going to make me?" taunted Franky. He hit Hubble with another.

Owen shoved Franky hard from behind, and knocked him to his knees. Rushing to Franky's defense, Fred jumped on Owen's back. Owen lost his balance, and they both came crashing down on top of Franky. Connie yanked Fred off Owen's back, while Franky and Owen began scuffling in the dirt.

In seconds Franky had straddled Owen, pinning his arms to the ground with his knees. "What are you going to do now, Baker?" he asked, raising his fist over Owen's face.

"*Grrrrrrrrrrrrrrrrrrrrrrrrr . . .*"

Franky felt hot dog-breath on his neck. He looked over his shoulder. Shep was showing his fangs and growling in his face. Franky froze. "Connie, isn't this *your* dog?" he asked, barely moving his lips.

"Yeah," said Connie, keeping a tight grip on Fred. "But *he's* not." She pointed her chin in Hubble's direction.

Franky turned and caught the wild, angry look in Hubble's eyes.

"*GRRRRRRRRRRRRRRRRRRRR . . .*" He growled even more ferociously than Shep.

"Help," squeaked Franky.

Barbara Ann and Nelly kept their eyes on Fred.

"Just bare your teeth, honey," instructed Barbara Ann.

"This really works?" asked Nelly.

"Every time," said Wilson.

"Call them off, Baker," cried Franky.

"Yeah, call them off," panted Fred.

"Hubble . . . It's okay, boy," said Owen.

Franky wanted to bolt.

"Just get up slowly," advised Owen.

"Those dogs bite us and my dad will sue," whined Franky.

"Give me the ball, Wilson," said Owen.

Wilson plopped the ball obediently in Owen's hand.

"Good boy," he said. He handed the ball to

Franky. "Here. But I bet they come after you for it."

The dogs stared at Franky and Fred with wild eyes. They growled and snapped their teeth hungrily.

"Keep it," said Franky. "I don't care."

"Is this your only one?" asked Owen.

"Just keep it," said Fred.

Owen shrugged. "Okay."

Connie laughed. Franky and Fred slunk away as fast as they dared.

"If we catch you without those dogs, Baker, you're dead meat," called Franky when they were a safe distance away.

"They're such total jerks," sighed Connie.

"Then why do you hang out with them?" asked Owen.

She shrugged. "I don't know. We just grew up together. I could hang with you, I guess."

"Don't let me force you," said Owen.

"No," said Connie. "I want to."

Owen smiled. Then he realized what it would

mean if she did. As per Hubble's orders—"the communication barrier must never be broken." How could he talk openly with the dogs when Connie was around? He looked at Hubble, who was under a tree licking his wounds.

"Um, would you keep an eye on the other dogs for a minute?" he asked her. "I want to check on Hubble."

"Sure," said Connie.

Carefully keeping his back to her, Owen knelt down by Hubble and whispered, "You all right?"

"I should have handled that on my own. Why did you step in like that?" asked Hubble.

"They were throwing rocks at you, Hub."

"Sirius dogs fight their own battles," declared Hubble. "Why would you put yourself at risk for me?"

"You're my dog—and that's what friends do," said Owen. "Besides, you backed me up too."

"I did, didn't I? Why would I do a stupid thing like that?"

As Owen left the scowling Hubble to ponder

his own questions, he noticed that the other dogs were staring at the ball in his hand.

"I think they want to play ball," said Connie.

"You want this?" Owen teased them. "Is this what you want?"

He gave the ball a long toss, and the crew tore off after it. They skidded and rolled and rammed into each other in their frenzy to get the prize. Hubble watched, fascinated.

"Why doesn't your dog play?" asked Connie.

"I'm not sure he knows how," said Owen.

Hubble flashed Owen an indignant look.

"Or maybe he's not good enough," Owen taunted.

Hubble sneezed and shook his ears.

"He does have allergies. . . ."

Hubble got up and woofed at them.

"Look, he wants to try," said Connie.

"Okay." Owen wound up for the big throw. "Go get it, boy!" he shouted.

The dogs tore off once again in hot pursuit. Hubble lagged behind, confused. Wilson caught the ball, raced back with it, and dropped it at Owen's feet. Owen threw the ball in the opposite direction this time, giving Hubble a little head start. "That's yours, Hub! All yours!" Owen shouted.

Hubble hesitated for a second, and the crew galloped over him like a herd of wild horses. He peeled himself off the ground and shook out his fur.

"You can do it," said Owen. "I know you can."

Barbara Ann returned and dropped the ball at Owen's feet.

"You show 'em, Hub. Show 'em what you're made of!" cried Owen, tossing the ball high and long.

Again Hubble trailed behind. But this time he stoked up the fire inside. He revved up his speed and leaped—soaring over the whole pack of dogs, over the ball. . . .

Connie and Owen stared at him in shock. The crew stopped in their tracks and stared too.

Wham! Hubble crashed down into the bushes

on the far side of the field.

"*Oof.*"

The dogs blinked for a moment in disbelief. Then they charged into the bushes, barking wildly in congratulation.

"Awesome, dude! You were flying! I want to try that. Me too! Where's the ball?" Owen could hear their exuberant comments.

"Is he all right?" asked Connie over the ruckus.

"He's fine," he said.

"Fine? He took off like a seven-forty-seven!" shouted Connie.

"Yeah, he's a good leaper," said Owen. "You know, like those dogs with the Frisbees?"

"Dogs don't fly!" cried Connie. "What is up with your dog?"

He hung his head. "You won't believe me."

Connie looked deep into his eyes and said, "I know how to keep a secret."

What could he do? She had seen Hubble flying. He might as well tell her the rest of the story now. With the crew in tow, he led her through the brushy woods to the hilltop where Hubble's spacecraft lay buried. Connie took it all in silently.

"If you tell anybody, Hubble could get in serious trouble. I mean . . . *Sirius* trouble." Owen pointed meaningfully to the sky.

Hubble grumbled. "You're the one in trouble, mister."

Owen ignored him.

Connie stared at Shep. "So . . . *he* talks to you too?"

"Yep. All the time."

"He . . . tells you stuff?"

Owen nodded.

Connie heard Shep woof something to Owen.

"He said, don't worry, he can keep secrets too."

Connie looked relieved.

Shep barked something else to Owen.

"Um, like how you think I'm cute," said Owen, embarrassed.

"SHEP!" cried Connie. She was mortified. But she was a believer now. No doubt about it!

CHAPTER 10

Hubble had certainly had better mornings than this one. He'd been hit with rocks, he'd crashed into bushes, failed at playing catch, and, basically, the dogs were no further along in their training than they were the day before. And as if all that were not bad enough, now his secret was out too!

He limped up to Owen's bedroom, fuming. As the door shut behind them, Hubble snapped, "We had an agreement—you weren't going to tell anybody about this!"

"Hey, don't blame me," cried Owen. "I'm not

the one who jumped five hundred feet right in front of her."

"I was just going for the ball," said Hubble.

"You were flying, Hubble! How'd you do that?"

"We have stronger gravity on Sirius. It's much bigger than Earth." Hubble winced in pain as he paced the room.

Owen looked at his favorite full-color NASA poster of Neil Armstrong. "Oh, so you're like an astronaut on the moon. You can jump higher and farther."

"I can do lots of things," barked Hubble. "What I *can't* do is catch that infuriating bouncy ball!"

Owen crouched down beside him. "Wait a second," he said. "That rock around your neck. Is that from outer space?"

"We all wear them—it's a token."

"What does it mean?

"It means . . . home," said Hubble. He sat down with a sigh.

"Here," said Owen, "lie down a minute."

"We have to work on the woofer. *Ooch*," groaned Hubble. He was so tired.

"We have time," said Owen, helping Hubble to his bed. "Just lay on your side."

"Why?" grumbled Hubble suspiciously.

"Would you just—"

Hubble plopped down, and Owen started rubbing his sore legs and joints.

"Oh, that's good," said Hubble.

"See?"

"You're a very nice person, Owen. I didn't know people could be so generous."

"Thank you. Now, *shhhh . . .*"

Hubble rolled on his back and Owen rubbed his belly.

"Okay. Oh, boy. Right there," said Hubble sleepily. "But we have to . . . work . . . woofer . . . *zzzzz . . .*"

He was out like a light.

Owen smiled. It was nice to have Hubble act like a pet—even if only this once.

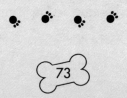

Back in their own homes, the crew dogs had completely forgotten their "training" and instead were trying to figure out how to fly. Owen's phone was ringing off the hook. Each time, it was another owner wondering why their dog was suddenly bouncing from chair to chair or leaping from high places. After the fourth phone call, Owen's parents were worried.

That evening they watched as Hubble and Owen limped over to the workshop. "And we thought a dog would make things easier," said his dad, dismayed. Mrs. Baker just shook her head in disbelief.

After hours of tinkering, Owen managed to get the woofer back in one piece. With a pair of tiny tweezers, he connected the last of the broken wires. A little red light began to glow on the side. But Owen and Hubble didn't notice.

"Did you see what my dad's building for you?" Owen asked.

Hubble sat beside the large, unpainted doghouse. But his attention was on the rubber ball at his feet. He batted it with his paw like a cat. "Huh?" he grunted at Owen absentmindedly.

"The doghouse," said Owen. "See, if you lived here, you'd get your very own digs."

The ball rolled back and bumped against Hubble's paw. "Digs?" Hubble pushed the ball away even harder.

"You know—house," explained Owen.

The ball rolled back. Hubble couldn't stand it anymore. He took off, chasing the thing across the shop. *Kablam!* Birdhouses and cans of paint went flying every which way.

Owen looked up from his work and laughed.

"*Pssssssshhhhhhhhhhhh . . . woooeeeeeeeooooooooo . . . shhhhhh . . .* Three-Nine-Four-Two." It was a weird voice coming from the woofer. "Three-Nine-Four-Two," it said through the static.

Owen reached for the woofer.

"Don't touch!" cried Hubble.

"Three-Nine-Four-Two . . . Three-Nine-Four-Two," the radio voice repeated more clearly.

"Must be some sort of code," mused Hubble.

"Aren't *you* Three-Nine-Four-Two?" asked Owen.

"Oh!" Hubble leaned toward the microphone. "Three-Nine-Four-Two here! I'm here. This is Three-Nine-Four-Two."

"Three-Nine-Four-Two, please respond," said the voice.

"I don't think they can hear you," said Owen.

"Visitation confirmed," continued the voice. "Arrival of the Greater Dane will be . . . *pssshhhh-hhhhhhhhhhhhhhhhhhhhhh . . .*"

"Arrival?" gasped Owen. He saw a look of panic in Hubble's eyes.

"Repeat. The Greater Dane will be arriving at transmitted coordinates on . . . *pssshhhhhhhhhhhh-hhhhh . . .*"

Owen grabbed the woofer. "When? When?" he cried.

Suddenly, his dad opened the door behind them. Owen whirled around and knocked the

The dogs take Owen for a walk.

Hubble teaches the Earth dogs to get Sirius!

Hubble is an out-of-this-world dog!

The dogs come to Owen's rescue.

Hubble and Owen have a talk.

Hubble's spaceship is destroyed.

This woofer couldn't get anyone's attention.

Time to move, *again*.

A close shave!

The Greater Dane means business.

The Greater Dane was not expecting a welcome like this.

The family, home for good.

Hooray for Earth dogs!

woofer to the floor. It crashed and broke into three pieces.

"Oops. What was that?" asked Mr. Baker.

"Nothing, it's nothing. It's okay," said Owen, desperately trying to appear calm.

"You all right?" asked his dad. "You look a little pale."

"I'm fine. Fine."

"Okay," said Mr. Baker. "Ten minutes till lights out."

Owen nodded. Mr. Baker slipped out, and Owen and Hubble stared at each other speechlessly. They opened the garage door and stepped out to look up at the stars.

"The Greater Dane is coming here," said Owen flatly.

"*Brrrrrr,*" Hubble shivered in terror.

"Is it really that bad?"

"Trust me, she is not going to be happy."

"She?" asked Owen. "The Greater Dane is a she?"

"Of course," said Hubble.

"Wow."

"We're doomed," said Hubble. "It's all over now."

"All over?"

"She's going to expect a royal welcome, a grand tour—"

"So, we'll do it," declared Owen. "We'll give it to her."

"You don't understand," said Hubble. "When she sees what I've seen here—she'll give the order."

"What order?"

"Owen . . ." Hubble hesitated.

"Tell me, Hub. What's the worst she can do?"

"Global recall," replied Hubble.

"Global what?"

"Recall." Hubble looked up to the sky. "All Earth dogs will be ordered back to Sirius for rehabilitation."

"*All* dogs?"

"Even the dingoes," said Hubble.

"She can't do that!" cried Owen.

78

"She *will* do that," said Hubble.

"I mean, *how* can she do that?" asked Owen.

"It'll be gradual," explained Hubble. "City by city. Day after day. But trust me, she *can*."

"I don't understand. Why *would* she?"

"I told you. This is a backward planet. Earth was supposed to have gone to the dogs ages ago."

From the garage door, Owen saw old Mr. Leone taking an evening stroll with his Nelly. What would humans do without their best friends?

"We can't let that happen, Hubble!" he cried.

"It won't be up to us," replied Hubble grimly.

"No. We can work with the dogs," said Owen. "You can teach them how to give the Greater Dane a royal welcome. Then we'll come up with something that shows her how dogs run things. I'll act like I'm *your* pet, if I have to."

"Fool the Greater Dane?" questioned Hubble. "She's got . . . instincts."

"Hubble, we *have* to try," cried Owen. "We can do this. I know we can!"

"You're just one boy, Owen," said Hubble gravely. "You can't save the world all on your own."

"I'm not trying to. But if you go away—and all the rest of the dogs go away—then . . . then . . ." Owen couldn't finish. His eyes welled with tears.

Hubble looked at him sympathetically. He was beginning to understand this human boy. He nodded knowingly and finished Owen's sentence: ". . . who's going to be your best friend?"

CHAPTER 11

Bright and early the next morning, the crew's emergency training began. Hubble lined them up at attention and started his lecture. This time there would be no time for meditation—the Greater Dane's spaceship was already on its way to Earth!

"When the Greater Dane arrives, we must welcome her with dignified pageantry," Hubble told them. "Your pride and honor should burst forth."

Right on cue, Shep let out one of his famous farts.

"Oh, Shep," sighed Barbara Ann.

"Sorry," muttered Shep. "Spaghetti and meatballs."

"Forget it. This is never going to work if you can't even *try* to act dignified!" Hubble ranted.

Connie and Owen watched.

"Hubble—" Owen tried to stop him.

"Not now, *I'm* yelling!" shouted Hubble. "You can't look *and* smell like a pack of idiots, you hear me? Not in front of her!"

The dogs lowered their heads in shame.

"What did he say?" whispered Connie.

"He's a little stressed out," said Owen.

Owen figured Hubble needed a break. "Let me talk to them a minute," he suggested. He knelt down at dog's-eye level. "You all understand you're being asked to prove yourselves, right? To prove that you're worthy to live here and stay with the people you love."

Shep looked up at Connie. "We want that

more than anything."

"We'll do whatever we need to do," said Nelly.

"I know you will," said Owen. "Just do your best."

The dogs nodded.

Owen turned back to Hubble. "They usually respond better to a little encouragement."

Hubble swallowed hard and collected himself. "Let's start over," he said calmly. "When the Dane passes, you must bow low before her. No one's head should ever be higher than hers. Let's practice. I'll play her."

Hubble paraded regally in front of his crew. As he passed, the dogs bowed gracefully, dropping their heads between their front paws.

"Thank you. Thank you, Earth dogs. Nice to see you," said Hubble, playing the part.

Owen and Connie got down on their hands and knees and bowed too.

"I am pleased to visit your fair planet," continued Hubble. He turned back to inspect the troops. Everyone was holding their bows perfectly.

"Not bad," he said.

Owen popped his head up. "Not bad? That was cool!"

"It *was* good, actually," agreed Hubble. "I want to 'encourage' you all to keep practicing. It's an attitude. Dignified. Sirius."

The dogs sat at attention—chests out, chins up.

Hubble turned to Owen. "Now, have you figured out a way to convince her that we're in charge?"

"Connie had an idea," said Owen.

"Well," said Connie, still a bit uncomfortable about the idea of conversing with dogs, "whenever a great leader visits the White House, they give a formal dinner."

Hubble cocked his head, interested.

"We could practice at my house," she suggested. "Owen and I could be your servants."

Hubble agreed.

Owen and Connie set the table for a royal banquet. They lit candles, put on classical music, and took out her grandmother's best china. The dogs struggled to seat themselves in the chairs with as much dignity as they could muster.

"I always wondered what the view was like from up here," mused Wilson.

"I'm not very good with heights," whined Nelly, balancing on two thick telephone books.

"This just feels right, doesn't it?" gushed Barbara Ann.

"What's on the menu?" asked Shep.

"Ahem," began Hubble, once again playing the regal part. "It's so lovely getting together like this, Earth dogs. We should do it more often."

"Well, it's hard for me, Your Majesty. I summer here, but I winter in Miami," said Barbara Ann in a breezy tone.

"Yes, I summer here too, but I winter in My-poopie," mocked Wilson.

Shep cracked up. Nelly laughed so hard she fell off her chair.

"Ahem," growled Hubble. "Bring on the first course!"

Dressed in crisp, white aprons, Owen and Connie carried out platters of cold cuts, leftover meats, chicken drumsticks, and beef bones.

Shep quivered. "I'm dreaming. Somebody pinch me!"

Wilson drooled and licked his lips. "Papa's gonna eat a new pair of shoes!"

Nelly and Barbara Ann looked as if they were about to pounce at any moment.

"Control. Con-trol," commanded Hubble.

The dogs held their places. Hubble nodded in approval.

Owen presented Hubble with a can of dog food for his inspection.

"Head lower," ordered Hubble.

Owen crouched ridiculously as he opened the can.

Connie tucked a clean white napkin in Wilson's collar and tried not to laugh.

Owen lowered a heaping spoonful of dog food

toward one of Hubble's bowls.

"Food left. Water right," Hubble corrected him.

Owen placed the food in the left-hand dish as ordered, giving a humble little bow when he'd finished. Connie carried the water pitcher over and filled Hubble's right-hand dish.

Hubble woofed at her.

"He's telling you to keep your head low," Owen explained.

"You're kidding me, right?" asked Connie.

Again Hubble barked.

Connie rolled her eyes and crouched lower.

"I must say, the humans are much more domesticated than I had expected," said Hubble, enjoying his regal role.

"It's hard to get good help these days." Wilson sighed.

Owen shot him a look.

"What are they saying?" asked Connie.

"You don't want to know," said Owen.

"I just adore canned food. Don't you, Your

Loyal Highness," said Barbara Ann, making conversation.

"You've got something in your teeth," said Hubble.

Owen wiped her teeth with a napkin. "Hubble," he asked, "has any Greater Dane ever visited Earth before?"

Hubble stared him down. *"We can't communicate, remember?"*

"Oops. Sorry," said Owen, bowing apologetically.

"It's been ages since the last visit," said Hubble.

"Well, I bet this'll be the fanciest welcome any Dane's ever gotten," cried Barbara Ann.

"Don't be so sure," warned Hubble. "Last time, everybody built her a bunch of pyramids."

Owen did a double take. But before he could tell Connie what Hubble had just said, they heard Connie's mom at the front door.

"Connie?" called Mrs. Fleming.

She set down her bag of groceries and stared in disbelief. "Please tell me that's not dog food on your grandmother's china!"

"*Eep!*" cried Connie.

Owen helped her clean up the canine feast and got the dogs ready to go home. "I hope she isn't too mad," he said.

"We might have to do the real thing at your house," said Connie. She bent down to Shep. "It'll be all right. Besides, it's worth it. Right, Shep? Gimme kisses. Gimme kisses."

Owen watched Hubble bristle at the sight of such an open display of affection. This was not a dog who was going to shower *him* with kisses any time soon!

As Connie and Owen said good-bye at the door, Franky and Fred rode past on their bikes.

"Any day now, Baker," threatened Franky. "You're going to get it."

"Hey, Connie," said Fred. "I think he likes you because you're a dog!"

They pedaled off, cackling like a couple of crows.

Connie rolled her eyes. "I told them I didn't

want to be friends anymore."

"Oh," said Owen.

"Franky said his dad was gonna stop giving my dad haircuts. Like that means anything. My dad's almost totally bald."

Owen and Connie laughed and laughed. What a wild day this had been!

CHAPTER 12

"I think they may actually have a chance," said Hubble as he and Owen meandered home. "If the welcome is proper, the Greater Dane could be swayed to go easy on them."

Owen felt his spirits soar. He pulled the rubber ball from his pocket. "Hey, look what I found," he teased.

All Sirius thoughts vanished from Hubble's mind. He wagged his tail and stared at the ball. "What is it about that thing? Throw it! Come on, throw it before I explode!" he barked.

"Go . . . get it!" cried Owen, faking a throw.

Hubble galloped down the street looking every which way for the ball. "I got it. I got it. . . . Where is it?"

He stopped and looked back at Owen, bewildered.

"Psych," said Owen. "It's called a fake-out."

"I don't like it," growled Hubble.

"Sorry." Owen smiled. This time he tossed the ball high and far.

Hubble bounded off after it. He leaped up . . . over . . . Too far! *Kablam!* Owen heard a row of garbage cans topple over like dominoes.

Hubble searched frantically among the clanking cans. "Lost it," he sighed.

Owen spotted the ball rolling into his own yard, where his parents were busy putting up a For Sale sign. His mom waved to him.

"Hey, hon!" she called. "It's going to be a big day tomorrow! We're going to sell, sell, sell!"

Owen's dad helped her attach a placard that said: OPEN HOUSE TOMORROW.

Owen nodded. His stomach flip-flopped and he felt his happiness vanish. He and Hubble climbed to their room, and Owen slumped on his bed.

Still preoccupied with the ball, Hubble muttered, "Focus. Eyes on the ball. I can do that."

"All right, Hub. Go to bed," sighed Owen.

"I'm just saying—I think I could get pretty good at this game."

"Well," said Owen, "what does it matter, if you're not going to be here long enough to play?"

"Oh. Right," said Hubble, pushing the ball away. He noticed Owen's gloomy mood. "Are you . . . agitated?"

"Yep. But it's not you, don't worry."

Hubble came to Owen's bed and offered him a biscuit.

"No, thanks," said Owen, holding back a smile. "Lights out."

Hubble headed to his own bed, circled it twice as usual, and settled in.

"All right, you've got to tell me!" cried Owen.

"What?"

"Why do you do those circles?"

Hubble thought a moment. "I'm building a mind fence," he said importantly.

"Excuse me?"

"A mind fence. It helps to keep out negative thoughts while you sleep," explained Hubble.

"Yeah, sure . . ." scoffed Owen.

"It works," cried Hubble. "How would you like to never *ever* have another bad dream?"

"Never?"

"Never ever."

Owen scowled at Hubble skeptically. He stood up on his bed and circled twice. He flipped off the lights and plopped back down to sleep. "There," he said. "Go to sleep."

Owen could hear Hubble chuckling in the darkness.

"Psych!" said Hubble.

Owen snapped the light back on and stared at him.

"Mind fence. I can't believe you fell for that one!" Hubble laughed.

Thwop! Owen beaned him on the head with a pillow. He flopped back in his bed, laughing out loud along with his crazy dog.

When they woke up next morning, Owen saw that his parents were ready to celebrate the open house. His dad had decorated the front porch with colorful balloons, and his mom had put fresh flowers in vases all around their perfectly arranged living room.

"What's an open house?" asked Hubble.

"People come in and poke around to see if they want to take over where you live," explained Owen.

"You should pee in every corner. That's what I'd do," said Hubble.

Owen was considering this when they heard his mom call up the stairs. "Owen? This is an all-family operation. Up and at 'em!'"

"Sorry, Ma," called Owen. "I've got to work with the dogs!"

She marched to his room, determined. "We need you around here today," she declared.

"Mom," pleaded Owen, "nothing's more important than me working with the dogs right now."

His mom let out a worried sigh and sat down on his bed. "Owen, we've gotten some interesting phone calls lately from the neighbors."

"Uh-huh . . ." said Owen, wondering what was coming next.

"A particularly interesting one last night from Connie's mother."

"Oh," said Owen.

"Honey, your dad and I think it's time to wrap it up with the neighborhood dogs. Just stick to Hubble for the time being."

"You don't understand, Mom," cried Owen. "The dogs need me now more than ever."

Mrs. Baker looked even more worried.

"Well . . ." She leaned over and kissed him. "Today you're needed here . . . with people."

"I could use a hand with this table, O," called his dad from the hallway.

As he helped his dad carry the kitchen table out to the backyard, Owen's mind raced. How was he going to escape from this and help the dogs?

Hubble milled around, underfoot.

"Dad, watch Hubble," cried Owen, "he's right under you."

Hubble trotted out of Mr. Baker's way, and Mrs. Baker nearly tripped over him as she carried a big platter of food out to the table.

Hubble barked and barked.

"Oh, that dog!" cried Mrs. Baker. "Not today, Hubba-bubba." She found Hubble's leash and tied him to one of the railings on the front porch.

"There." She patted his head. "You sit nicely out here and say 'Hello! It's open house day! Buy, buy, buy!'"

On their bikes at the curb, Franky and Fred watched the frantic activities of the Baker household. There was Owen's weird dog, tied to the front porch all alone. Franky and Fred grinned at each other. This was the opportunity they'd been waiting for!

While Owen and his mom and dad were busy putting an awning up over the table in the back, Franky and Fred sauntered over to their front porch. . . .

"That should do it," said Mr. Baker as he and Owen finished tying the awning down.

"Looks good," agreed Owen.

Then, from somewhere far off, they heard a loud, earth-shaking BOOM!

"Whoa!" cried Mr. Baker.

"What was that?" asked Owen, even though he was pretty sure he had heard that sound before.

"Sounded like a sonic boom," said Mr. Baker.

Mrs. Baker stepped out of the house and viewed the table and the awning with delight. She snapped a picture. "My heroes!" she cried.

"*That* was a sonic boom?" asked Owen.

"Owen," said Mrs. Baker, "change that shirt— I need you to pass out fact folders to the guests."

Mr. Baker looked at Owen, still puzzling. "Maybe," he said. "I used to hear them when I was a kid, but we lived near an air force base."

"Owen, ticktock!" reminded Mrs. Baker.

"Okay, okay . . ." Owen headed inside and put on a new shirt. He picked up the pile of "fact folders" his mom had designed and went out to the porch to greet visitors. As soon as he was outside he noticed Hubble's leash—it was dangling from the porch railing—and Hubble was gone!

"Mom!" called Owen.

In the living room, his mom was introducing herself to some guests.

"Mom?" he called again.

"There you are!" she crooned. "Honey, the folders." She handed one to each of the guests.

"I can't find Hubble," whispered Owen urgently. "He's not out front."

"Feel free to roam the house as you like," she said breezily to the guests. "I'm sure he's around here somewhere, hon," she whispered back to Owen.

Owen shook his head. He ran out back and scanned the backyard. He ran to the front porch. Another guest was approaching. Owen faked a smile and said, "Here. Have a folder." He handed him the whole stack and took off running.

Owen pounded on Connie's door. "Hubble's gone!" he cried when she appeared.

"Is the Greater Dane here?" she asked.

"I don't know," panted Owen. "We've got to find Hubble."

Connie and Owen gathered the crew quickly and explained the situation. "We need all of your noses!" declared Owen.

CHAPTER 13

Down the street near the barbershop, Hubble was being held prisoner. Franky and Fred had tied a burlap sack over his head, and they were walking—Hubble had no idea where. He struggled to escape, but Fred held him tight.

Franky climbed into the shop through the back window. "Hand him over," he called to Fred.

Fred passed Hubble up through the window and then climbed in himself.

"Let's give him a close shave!" cried Franky, shaking up a can of shaving cream.

"Yeah!" agreed Fred with a devilish laugh.

Poor Hubble trembled inside the dark sack.

But Shep, Barbara Ann, Wilson, and Nelly were already on Hubble's trail. Sniffing and woofing, they pulled Owen and Connie toward the barbershop. Owen whispered to them to quiet down as they approached the front window. He peeked inside. "Oh, no," he groaned. He could see Fred holding Hubble down in one of the barber chairs. Hubble was covered in shaving cream!

Owen tried the door. Locked! He banged on the window. "Leave him alone!" he shouted.

As Fred and Franky turned to see who was at the window, Hubble shook the bag off his head and jumped from the chair. Fred tried to grab him again, but Hubble snapped at his hands.

"Ow!" cried Fred, losing his grip.

Hubble headed for the back window.

"Get him!" cried Franky.

They tried to run, but they slipped on the shaving cream and flopped on the floor.

Hubble bounded out the window. The boys

scrambled to their feet and chased down the alley after him.

Suddenly, Franky and Fred stopped cold.

"*Grrrrrrrrr!*" At the end of the alley, Wilson, Nelly, Shep, and Barbara Ann were lined up, shoulder-to-shoulder, growling at them. Connie and Owen stood behind them, their faces set in determination.

"Run!" cried Franky.

"*Ahhhhhhhhhhhhhhh!*" screamed Fred.

The boys took off in the opposite direction, with the crew in hot pursuit.

"Help!" cried Fred as the dogs chased them down Owen's street.

Soon, Wilson and Shep took the lead and cut them off, herding them into Owen's driveway. Barbara Ann and Nelly rushed in to help. Owen and Connie hurried to catch up.

Terrified, Franky and Fred dove into Owen's garage. The dogs leaped in behind them. The boys threw birdhouses and paint cans on the floor, trying to block the dogs' way. But the crew kept coming. They dashed around Mr. Baker's work-table and back toward the side door.

Kablam! As he rushed for the door, Franky knocked over Mr. Baker's canister of paint sealant. *Hisssssssssssssssssssssssss* . . . The canister began leaking toxic fumes!

The dogs screeched to a halt just before crashing into the rolling canister themselves. Seizing the opportunity, the boys bolted out the door and slammed it shut. The crew was trapped inside with the poisonous gas!

As the dogs barked at them from the garage window, Franky and Fred took cover under the bushes near the driveway.

Breathing hard, Owen finally turned into his driveway and scanned his yard for the dogs.

Just behind him, Connie stopped short and stared. "You're moving?" she asked.

"What? Oh, yeah . . ." said Owen.

"When were you going to tell me?" asked Connie.

"I don't know." Owen shrugged helplessly.

Before he could explain, they heard faint barking from the garage. Connie flung the side door open, and the dogs spilled out in a gray cloud of fumes. Coughing and sputtering, they made a beeline for the bushes.

Franky and Fred leaped out and dashed into Owen's house with the crew hot on their heels. In Mrs. Baker's perfect living room, vases crashed, chairs toppled, and pictures fell from the walls as the dogs, still loopy from the fumes, thundered through, trying to apprehend the kidnappers.

"*Aaahhhhhhhhhhhh!*" cried Fred.

"Help!" cried Franky.

They ran out the back door, just missing the buffet table and whizzing past the startled guests. Right behind them, the dogs bumped and jostled each other in wild confusion.

Owen and Connie hardly dared look at the scene in the backyard. Owen spotted his parents standing wide-eyed in disbelief.

Franky and Fred doubled back and dove

under the table, pulling the tablecloth down with them. A beautiful lemon meringue pie flew off the table and landed on Hubble's head.

The guests gasped. Gobs of meringue dripped slowly down over Hubble's eyes. Wilson, Shep, Barbara Ann, and Nelly stopped to stare at Hubble, but the fumes had made them so dizzy they could hardly stay on their feet.

"GRRRRRRRRRRRRRRRRRRR."
A weird, unearthly growl made them freeze. Everyone turned at once to see the sun glinting off the steely gray coat of an enormous Great Dane.

Connie and Owen exchanged a glance. There was no doubt about it—the Greater Dane had arrived.

The dogs began to tremble in fear.

Hubble blinked. A blob of meringue slid off one eye, and the awful truth became clear to him.

The Dane tossed her head back regally and surveyed the disaster.

Owen and Connie dropped to their knees and

bowed. "Mom, Dad?" whispered Owen. "Bow down."

"What?" they cried.

Suddenly, the Dane's henchman, a little Chinese Crested dog, trotted forward, yapping orders. The wobbly crew dogs tried their best to stand at attention.

Seeing everyone distracted by the Dane, Franky nudged Fred and cried, "Go! Go!"

They popped out from under the table. Fred's foot hit a puddle of lemon meringue pie and he slipped. As he fell backward he reached out for the table, but caught the edge of a food tray instead. A big bowl of macaroni salad went catapulting through the air.

All eyes followed the salad as it went up, up, up . . . and then down, *splat*, all over the Greater Dane's head.

Owen covered his mouth in horror. Connie covered her eyes. Franky and Fred fled.

"Coffee and cake inside, everybody!" announced Owen's mom bravely. She shot Owen a stern glance as she led her guests to safety.

The Greater Dane shook herself grandly. Macaroni flew off in all directions.

"What's the matter with all of you," squeaked her henchman. "Don't you know who this is? Look smart!"

"Get in line, quick! I can't see straight. I can't stop giggling. It's not funny. What was in that gas?" The dogs yapped at one another, trying to collect themselves.

Hubble wobbled up to the Dane and performed a shaky bow. "Your Majesty. You are my humble servant," he tried. "No, wait, that's not right. . . ."

"You have a lot of explaining to do, Three-Nine-Four-Two," boomed the Dane.

"Right, Three-Nine-Four-Two . . . that's my number. Don't wear it out!" Hubble giggled. "I'm sorry, okay, I'm totally serious now. Oops, Sirius!" He buried his nose in his paws and laughed uncontrollably.

"Pull yourself together, Canid," barked the

Dane. She cast a disapproving glance over the dogs who were lined up in their crooked row. "Isn't there one among you who knows how to give your leader a proper welcome?"

One of Shep's farts exploded. The crew froze in a panic. "Heh . . ." Wilson tried to stifle a giggle. And then all hope of dignity was lost—the dogs fell on top of one another in one great laughing heap.

"*Rrrrrrrrrrrrrrrrrrrrrrrrrrr*," rumbled the Dane.

Owen moaned. He could hardly stand to look.

"This couldn't get any worse," groaned Connie.

Suddenly Bob, the dogcatcher, raced in to the rescue! With one quick swing he swung the loop of his brace stick over the Dane's head and tightened it around her neck. "Gotcha!" he cried.

"Oh, yeah, it could," said Owen.

CHAPTER 14

Owen and Hubble peered down the long row of cages at the animal shelter. In the big one at the far end, the Dane and her little henchman barked furiously.

"You know, we could just leave her here," suggested Hubble.

"Hubble . . ."

"What? She might get adopted, move in with a nice family, have a good life . . ."

Owen gave him a doubtful look.

" . . . and never rest until she hunts me down

and kills me," finished Hubble. "Okay, let's spring her."

"They're new clients—just need more training," Owen explained to Bob. "I'll take them straight home."

Bob helped Owen put collars and leashes on the new dogs, and Owen led them out.

Once outside, they met Connie and the crew, and the Dane took them to her super-sleek, ultramodern spaceship parked on the hillside near Hubble's crash site. The dogs plopped down under the old oak tree, their heads drooping. They braced themselves for the Dane's decision.

"Every rumor I'd heard about our species on this planet appears to be true," she began. "No dominance. No dignity."

"We *had* something planned for you," tried Hubble.

"I've seen all I need to see, Three-Nine-Four-Two," she replied.

"No, you haven't!" interrupted Owen.

The Dane turned to him with great indignation.

Owen struggled for the right words. "You haven't. You can't take them away. Please. Dogs mean so much to the world, and you haven't seen any of that yet. Dogs help sick people and they work with firefighters and police and do amazing things—things people could never do on their own. They protect us and keep us company and they always warn us if something bad might happen. Some dogs even help guide people who can't see. We rely on them for so much, and you should be proud of them. Because people *love* dogs, did you know that? People and dogs love one another."

The Dane shot Owen a withering glance. "I'm still curious as to why a human boy is *talking* with me," she said to Hubble.

"Heh," laughed Hubble sheepishly. "Funny story . . ."

"*You* did this?" she barked.

Hubble lowered his head.

"It isn't Hubble's fault. I mean, Three-Nine-Four-Two," cried Owen. "It's not his fault."

The Dane rumbled in irritation.

"You'd better step down, Owen," whispered Hubble.

"I'm sorry. But please think about what I said." Owen left the hilltop so the Dane could talk to the dogs in private.

She turned to Hubble and sighed grandly. "Breaking *all* the rules, are we?"

From the base of the hill, Connie and Owen watched as the Dane lectured the dogs. Then the crew huddled together with Hubble and talked for a while among themselves.

"What happened?" asked Owen when they came down.

"She's going home," replied Hubble.

"Really? Is it over?" Owen asked.

"It's all over," said Hubble.

"Yes!"

"You did it, Owen. You convinced her," said Connie.

"Did I? Wait, what about you, Hubble?" asked Owen. "Are you . . . here?"

"I'm here."

"I don't believe it. I thought I blew it. That's great, isn't it?" gushed Owen. "Where's everybody going?"

The dogs were silent.

"I think everyone's tired," said Hubble.

Owen glanced up the hill. The Dane and her henchman were climbing aboard their spaceship. "Oh. That makes sense," he said. "We can celebrate later, right?"

Back at home that evening, Owen helped a very quiet Hubble into a warm bath. "We can play ball now, Hub—and I'm a real good coach," he said as he shampooed lemon pie out of Hubble's fur. "I know it's not easy *not* going back to Sirius. But it seems like life is so much harder there."

Hubble looked like a poor, sad stray who'd been out in the rain too long.

"And everybody deserves a chance to be happy, right?" continued Owen. He dried Hubble with a big towel. "Time for bed."

Hubble circled his bed twice slowly while Owen got into his pajamas and closed the bedroom door.

"Could you leave that open?" asked Hubble. "It's warm tonight."

"Sure," said Owen.

Hubble's eyes followed Owen's every movement.

"What?" asked Owen.

"I know . . . I haven't been the most affectionate . . . companion," Hubble stammered.

"It's all right. You're different, Hub. I like that about you," said Owen.

"But I've seen the way dogs express themselves to their people . . . and . . ."

"Are you talking about doggie kisses?"

"I want you to know I do like you. I'm just not used to all the customs here."

"Hubble, it's okay. You just told me you like

me. How many people get to hear that from their dog?"

Hubble looked up at Owen like a devoted pet might look at his beloved human. Owen smiled and switched off the light.

When he was sure Owen had fallen asleep, Hubble crept out of bed. He spotted the rubber ball, picked it up in his teeth, laid it gently at the foot of Owen's bed, and tiptoed away. Quietly, he pushed his nose against the doggie flap in the kitchen and slipped out into the dark, drizzly night.

In the street, Shep, Wilson, Barbara Ann, and Nelly were already gathering. They had said their sad, silent good-byes to their people that evening. They were ready.

Hubble led them down the familiar path— through the brushy woods to the hillside.

CHAPTER 15

The next morning dawned gloomy and gray. Owen awoke to the sound of his mother's voice calling him. She sounded worried.

"Huh?" he asked, rubbing the sleep from his eyes.

"Honey, Ms. Ryan is at the door. She'd like to speak with you," Mrs. Baker said.

"What about?"

Owen saw Hubble's empty bed. As he got up, the rubber ball dropped to the floor and rolled under his dresser. He pulled on some clothes and

117

went to the door as quickly as he could.

Ms. Ryan looked frantic. "It's as if she's simply vanished!" she cried.

Owen's mind raced. What were those dogs up to? He saw Wilson's "dad" and Mr. Leone coming down the walkway. And they looked worried too.

Before they could say a word, Owen took off out the door. "I'll find them!" he called over his shoulder as he ran.

Connie was already on the hilltop under the old oak tree when Owen arrived. They stared at the ground where Hubble's spaceship had crashed. But the only thing there was an empty hole and a pile of dirt.

"Oh, no," Owen groaned.

"No one will believe us now," Connie sighed.

They shuffled back home through the quiet streets. There wasn't a dog barking anywhere.

"There must be something we can do," said Connie.

"Communicate with them," said Owen. "That's all we *can* do. I need to say the right things to convince the Dane she's making a mistake."

The next day, Owen carried the three pieces of the broken woofer up to his room and laid them on his desk. He made a list of supplies he needed and headed for Connie's house.

"I'm going to the hardware store to get some more wires and stuff," he said. "Want to come along?"

Connie's mother called to her and gave her a meaningful look.

"Um . . . I can't," stammered Connie.

Owen could tell by Mrs. Fleming's face that he was no longer a welcome visitor. Sadly, he went home.

What did the grown-ups think of him now? Owen wondered. Did they think he had done something terrible with their dogs? Did they think he was crazy? All alone, he tinkered with the woofer on his desk. He studied wiring diagrams for Earth receivers. He tried everything. Still, nothing seemed to work.

His mom and dad sold their house a few days later. They began packing up dishes and clothes. Down in the garage, Owen's dad painted over Hubble's name on the new doghouse. Hubble had never gotten to use it.

In his room, surrounded by boxes packed with clothes and toys, Owen sat with his head slumped down next to the woofer. He'd worked frantically for days. He was exhausted, and he was running out of time. "I'm doing something wrong," he muttered to himself. "I'm missing something."

Bling! Owen lifted his head. It was an instant message coming in from Connie on his computer.

"Any luck yet?" she was asking.

"Nope. Nothing," typed Owen.

"Keep working. Don't freak out, but my dad said some people at his job have lost their dogs too."

Owen read Connie's words on his screen and tried hard not to panic.

At her house, Connie heard a knock at the door. "Connie?" her mom called.

"Oops, gotta go," she said, quickly signing off.

Owen thought about what Connie's message might mean. He thought about what Hubble had said—"Global Recall." He leaned over to his telescope and surveyed the stars. Just to the left of the moon he saw Sirius—the Dog Star. He wondered how much time he had before every dog on Earth was gone.

CHAPTER 16

Owen's mom carried a pizza box into the kitchen and flipped on the evening news. She called to Owen, who was sitting at his desk staring blankly at the woofer. He came downstairs looking awful. Too many sleepless nights had worn him ragged.

"The movers will be loaded up and leaving here by ten tomorrow," she told him, gently smoothing back his hair. "Where's your orange cap?"

"I can't find it," said Owen.

"Honey, you know we'll get you another dog,"

she said. "And soon. That's a promise."

"Maybe I'm not supposed to have one, Mom," said Owen.

"Don't say that. Nobody deserves a dog more than you." She kissed him on the cheek.

Before they could take a bite of their pizza, the news anchor's excited voice coming from the TV caught their attention: "File this under 'odd.' There's been a drastic increase in reports of lost dogs all over the state recently. Authorities are baffled by the rash of disappearances, but say they are doing their best to 'sniff out' the culprits."

"That *is* odd," said Mrs. Baker.

Owen wolfed down a slice of pizza and hurried to the garage. He didn't have a moment to lose! He remembered knocking the woofer onto the floor. Maybe, just maybe, there was another part they had missed. He got down on his hands and knees and searched the floor. He peered into every dark corner and under every low cabinet. Then, beneath an old dresser, he found a small metal fuse. *This must be it!* he thought.

He went back to his room and clicked the fuse into place. The woofer just sat there. The wires had to be connected perfectly. Owen went back to work.

Outside his window, the neighbors were talking with his parents.

"It's hard to understand how he could know *nothing* about what happened," said Wilson's "dad."

"He spent more time with those dogs than anyone," added Ms. Ryan.

"And now you're moving away?" whined Mrs. Fleming. "Where does that leave all of us?"

Connie overheard what the grown-ups were saying. "It's not Owen's fault," she said.

"Connie, go inside," said Mr. Fleming gravely.

"Owen tried to stop them, but he couldn't," she explained.

"Stop who, Connie?" asked Mr. Baker. "Who took them?"

"Dogs. The *other* dogs," said Connie, gathering

her courage. "From outer space."

The adults shook their heads sadly. "Maybe it is best you're leaving," said Mr. Fleming.

When the neighbors had gone, Owen's mom sighed. "It's because of all this constant moving, isn't it?"

"I'm sure it doesn't help," said his dad.

"The deal on the house hasn't officially closed yet. It's not too late to change our minds."

"I thought you wanted to get started on the new place right away," said Mr. Baker.

"On the other hand, how's he going to get along here now?" sighed Mrs. Baker. "What do we do?"

"Only our best," said Mr. Baker. "And trust our instincts."

As his parents lay awake worrying and wondering, Owen worked on the woofer. It was after midnight already. His hands trembled and he could hardly see the wires through his tears. With one last flicker of hope, he finished connecting the fuse. Nothing.

"Hubble, I'm sorry," cried Owen hopelessly. "I should have kept quiet on that hill."

The red light on the side of the woofer began to glow. But Owen had closed his tired, teary eyes. "I'm sorry if I got you in trouble by talking." Whether or not anyone was listening, Owen felt he had to say the words. "I didn't think of . . . I just didn't think. Now everyone's losing their dogs, and it's all my fault." He wiped his eyes on his sleeve.

"I know you can't hear me, but I miss you so much. I never had a friend like you, and I wanted you to stay with me so badly, but I . . ."

He took a deep breath and continued bravely. He wished, somehow, Hubble could hear him. "I know you have your home there, and I hope I didn't screw everything up for you. I hope they're not being mean to you. Because you're a good boy. You are, Hubble."

CHAPTER 17

Light-years away, Hubble sat next to a huge
woofer with a glowing red light.

"You are—you're a good boy. . . ." Hubble sat
at attention. His left ear unfolded. That was
Owen's voice!

The Greater Dane loomed behind him. She
considered Owen's message. "I've often wondered
what it was about human beings that could lead
so many of our species astray—what is it that
makes us abandon our drive for dominance?"

Hubble hung his head.

"Go on, Three-Nine-Four-Two," she demanded. "Speak. Enlighten me."

"I think . . . it's friendship," mused Hubble. "People and dogs work side by side on Earth. And they make a home together."

"A home," she pondered. "It seems that inspires great loyalty."

Hubble nodded.

"I must ask you now. Where does *your* loyalty lie?"

Hubble thought for a while.

"Three-Nine-Four-Two?"

Finally sure of himself, Hubble sighed and said calmly, "I prefer the name Hubble."

CHAPTER 18

The moving van pulled up outside Owen's house at dawn. In his room, Owen packed a few last things—Hubble's toys, the rubber ball, the doggie bed. He looked around for anything he might have forgotten. Under the bed he spotted his orange baseball cap. He slapped it against his thigh to shake off the dust bunnies, and Hubble's rock fell out. Owen smiled. *He must have left this for me,* he thought, wrapping the string around his wrist.

Owen's mom and dad watched the movers

load the last of the boxes onto the truck.

"You'll follow us," Owen's dad told the driver. "It's about an hour."

"Owen? It's time, hon!" called his mom.

Owen straightened his orange cap and came outside. He saw Connie standing near the van.

"I guess this is it," he said to her.

"You'd better e-mail me," said Connie. She hugged him.

"Bye," said Owen sheepishly.

Behind him the movers were getting ready to close the truck's back door. *Kablam!* Owen jumped. "Dad? Was that another sonic boom?" he asked.

"No, O. No, that was just the movers shutting the door."

His mom motioned for them to climb into the car. "We really need to get going!"

As they pulled out of the driveway, Owen turned and saw Franky and Fred on their bikes, sneering at him. Along the street, Ms. Ryan and

Wilson's "dad" had also stepped out to watch them go. Around the corner, Mr. Leone was waving good-bye.

Owen was crushed. He had lost his dog, and now he was losing his first real friend. And, soon, all the dogs in the world would vanish, and there was not one thing he could do about it. He sank down in the backseat and sighed.

Suddenly, the car hit a pothole in the road. *BOOM!*

"Dad!" cried Owen.

"Sorry about that," said Mr. Baker. "Pothole."

"No, that was too big a noise," said Owen.

"Owen . . ." Mr. Baker protested.

Owen craned his neck to get a view of the sky. "That *was* too big a noise!" He looked down at the rock hanging from his wrist. Something was happening. He knew it!

"Dad, stop. Wait!" he cried.

"What is it?" asked Mrs. Baker.

"Stop the car!" cried Owen. "I forgot something!"

"What?" asked Mr. Baker.

There was no way to explain. Owen opened the car door. His dad screeched on the brakes.

"Owen?" cried Mrs. Baker, trying to stop him.

Owen stumbled into the street, barely dodging out of the way of the moving van and the oncoming cars. He ran back up his street, past his neighbors, past Connie. . . .

"What're you doing?" she called.

"Follow me!" he cried over his shoulder as he ran.

She took off after him, and in a moment she knew what it was. "The dogs! The dogs!" she shouted to the neighbors.

The Bakers left their car on the street and came running. Franky and Fred, Mr. Leone and Ms. Ryan, the Flemings and Wilson's "dad" followed too.

Owen and Connie headed for the path through the brushy woods.

"I know I heard it, I know it . . ." panted Owen.

They raced up the hillside to the old oak tree. Owen searched the skies. "Please, please," he pleaded. "Where are you?" He waited and waited.

At the bottom of the hill a crowd of grown-ups had gathered. He felt their worried stares upon him. Then, suddenly, their expressions changed—they were looking up at the sky in shock.

It was Hubble's spacecraft!

Owen raised his arms and whooped for joy. "Hubble!" he shouted.

Hubble maneuvered his craft in an elegant arc over the treetops. Owen waved him on. "Come on, boy! C'mere, boy!" he called. Hubble swooped down over Owen's head. *Too fast*, thought Owen.

Crunch! Hubble zoomed past the hilltop and crashed into the woods.

A big plume of smoke rose up. Owen thought he could hear familiar voices through the coughing and sputtering.

"See?" Wilson was saying. "You should've let me drive."

"Phew . . . such a smell of sulfur," complained Barbara Ann.

"That's the last time I travel in a spaceship," declared Nelly.

"Anyone else's butt fall asleep?" growled Shep.

One by one the crew dogs staggered out of the smoke and trotted up to Owen.

"We're home!" cried Nelly.

"There's my main man!" shouted Wilson.

"Who's hungry?" joked Shep.

Soon they were jumping all over Owen excitedly, showering him with doggie kisses. He hugged them and petted every one.

"Do I still look lovely?" asked Barbara Ann.

"You all look great," said Owen.

"They weren't so smart up there," said Nelly.

"Yeah, all work and no play," complained Wilson.

"I missed people food," cried Shep.

"I missed *people*!" cried Barbara Ann.

The others woofed in agreement.

"Well, they're right over there. They'll be real

happy to see you." Owen led the dogs over the crest of the hill. When they spotted their people, they ran and leaped into their arms.

Connie wrapped Shep in a big hug, and he covered her face with kisses. Beaming, she gave Owen a big thumbs-up.

Owen stood alone on the hilltop. His neighbors looked up at him with new appreciation. His mom and dad looked at him, worried, wondering if Hubble would appear too.

Owen peered into the woods. And then he spotted him! Hubble stepped away from the wreck and looked up at Owen meekly. Owen smiled.

EEERRRK, CRASH, THUMP! A big teetering limb fell down and demolished what was left of the spacecraft.

Hubble cringed, embarrassed.

"I really missed you," cried Owen.

"I know," Hubble said quietly. "I heard."

"You heard?

Hubble nodded. "I think you're a good boy too."

Owen laughed. He looked over his shoulder at the crash. "Are you . . . here to stay?"

Hubble nodded again. "The Greater Dane declared Earth dogs an entirely different breed. She's sending us all back home."

"Hmmm," said Owen, "impressive decision."

BZZZZZZZZZZZZZZZZZZZZZTTTTT . . . A weird buzzing noise came from the woods.

"Well, she had one condition," said Hubble.

Back on Sirius, the Greater Dane sat in her control room with her paw regally poised. She reached toward the control panel and pressed a big red button.

Z Z Z Z Z Z Z Z a a a a a p p p! Crrrrrrraaaaaaakkkkkkk! A huge blinding flash of light streamed down from the sky above Hubble's spacecraft and engulfed the hilltop.

"Whoa!" cried Owen. He blinked, trying to get used to normal light again. "Was that your woofer?"

Hubble panted happily.

"Hubble?" Owen looked into his eyes.

Hubble stared back and panted some more.

"But I have so many questions to ask you," said Owen. "How am I going to know what you're thinking?"

Hubble lowered his head and kissed Owen's hand. He looked up into Owen's eyes.

Owen smiled.

Then Hubble stood and put his front paws on Owen's shoulders. For the first time ever, he covered Owen's face in doggie kisses, knocking his orange cap right off his head in his excitement.

Owen's parents put their arms around one another and watched, delighted. "What should we tell the movers?" asked his dad.

"Start unpacking," cried his mom. "We're home for good!"

The next morning, Owen awoke to the buzz of his Snoopy alarm clock in his old familiar room. He slapped Snoopy's off button.

What day is this? he wondered.

He looked in the corner at the pile of dog toys. *Dog. Do I have a dog? Or was it all a dream?* he asked himself.

Then Hubble poked his head around the corner of the bed. He held the rubber ball in his mouth and looked up at Owen hopefully.

Owen grinned. Time for work! He pulled on his maroon uniform. He strapped on his utility belt and checked the mirror to make sure his cap was straight.

As usual, he picked up Barbara Ann first, then Wilson, Nelly, and Shep. This time Connie couldn't wait to walk the dogs with him.

At the park, Owen teased the crew. "You want this? You want it?" he cried, waving the ball under their noses. He sent a long toss high across the field, and the dogs took off, woofing and leaping wildly for the prize. But none of them—not Wilson, or Nelly, or Shep, or Barbara Ann—could ever leap higher or farther than Hubble!